This book is for Kaleb—whose missing fart inspired it all—and for the Game Night Crew, who are always willing to spend several hours engaged in a deep, meaningful discussion about farts.

STERLING CHILDREN'S BOOKS and the distinctive Sterling Children's Books logo are registered trademarks of Sterling Publishing Co., Inc.

ISBN 978-1-4549-1954-4

Library of Congress Cataloging-in-Publication Data
Names: Kelley, Marty, author, illustrator.
Title: Almost everybody farts / by Marty Kelley.
Description: New York : Sterling Children's Books, [2017] | Summary: Drawings paired with rhyming text depict the farting of many types of people and animals.
Identifiers: LCCN 2016035334 | ISBN 9781454919544
Subjects: | CYAC: Stories in rhyme. | Flatulence--Fiction. | Humorous stories.
Classification: LCC PZ8.3.K298 AI 2017 | DDC [E]--dc23 LC record available at https://lccn.loc.gov/2016035334

Distributed in Canada by Sterling Publishing Co., Inc.
c/o Canadian Manda Group, 664 Annette Street
Toronto, Ontario, Canada M6S 2C8
Distributed in the United Kingdom by GMC Distribution Services
Castle Place, 166 High Street, Lewes, East Sussex, England BN7 1XU
Distributed in Australia by NewSouth Books
45 Beach Street, Coogee, NSW 2034, Australia

For information about custom editions, special sales, and premium and corporate purchases, please contact Sterling Special Sales at 800-805-5489 or specialsales@sterlingpublishing.com.

Manufactured in China

Lot #:
10
11/20

sterlingpublishing.com

Design by Julia Morris

MARTY KELLEY used to be a second grade teacher, but now he's an author, an illustrator, and a drummer in the world's greatest children's music band (if he does say so himself). He lives in a fart-proof fortress in New Hampshire with his wife and his two teenage kids. When he's not busy making books or drumming, Marty visits lots of schools to talk about writing and illustrating.
martykelley.com

Almost
EVERYBODY
FARTS

Marty Kelley

STERLING CHILDREN'S BOOKS
New York

Grandmas
fart.

Teachers fart.

Terrifying creatures **fart**.

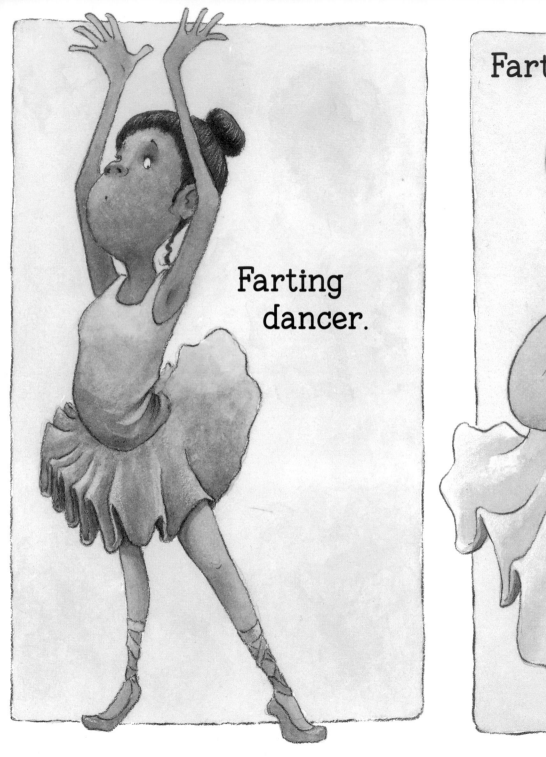

Farting
dancer.

Farting singer.

Farts when Dad says, "Pull my finger."

Sisters fart.

Brothers fart.

Sometimes even mothers f—

No.

Mothers do not **fart**.

Dainty little fairies **fart.**

Farts like
fire.

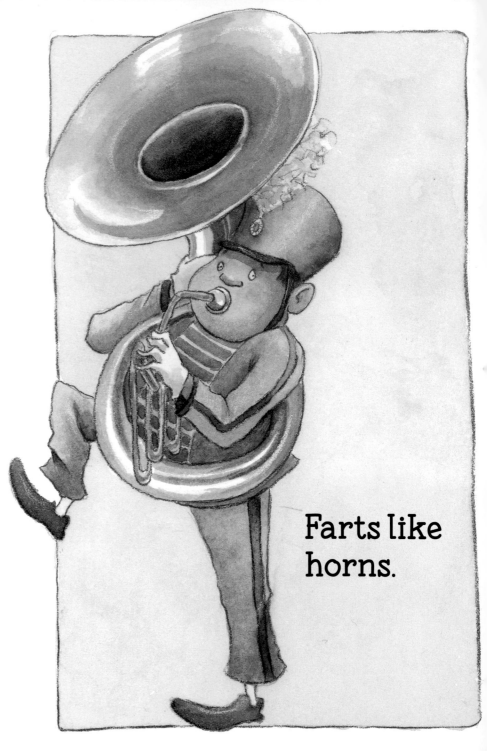

Farts like
horns.

Rainbow farts
from unicorns.

One fart.

Another fart.

I think I heard your mother f—

No.

Mothers do not fart.

Clowns fart.

Cooks fart.

People reading books **fart.**

Breaking wind.

Cut the cheese.

Ninja farts

are SBDs.

Silent farts.

Drama farts.

And, really. Yes. Your mama f—

No.

Mothers do not **fart**.

Farting poodle.

Farts
in school.

Farts make bubbles in the pool.

Farting chicken.

Farting bunny.

Uncles **fart** and think it's funny.

Farts that whisper.

Farts that roar.

Someone's **farting** behind that door!

Everybody farts.